Felicity
the Friday
Fairy

For Danielle Cropley
with lots of love

Special thanks to
Narinder Dhami

No part of this work may be reproduced, stored in a retrieval system, or transmitted in any form or by any means, electronic, mechanical, photocopying, recording, or otherwise, without written permission of the publisher. For information regarding permission, write to Rainbow Magic Limited c/o HIT Entertainment, 830 South Greenville Avenue, Allen, TX 75002-3320.

ISBN-10: 0-545-06760-X
ISBN-13: 978-0-545-06760-7

12 11 10 9 8 7 6 5 4 3 2   8 9 10 11 12 13/0

Printed in the U.S.A.

First Scholastic printing, August 2008

Felicity
the Friday
Fairy

by Daisy Meadows

SCHOLASTIC INC.

New York Toronto London Auckland Sydney
Mexico City New Delhi Hong Kong Buenos Aires

The Fairyland Palace

Time Tower

Windy Lake

Tippingt Tow

Morristown Aquarium

The Tall Toy Store

Fashi F

Fountain

Dancing Days

Tow Ha

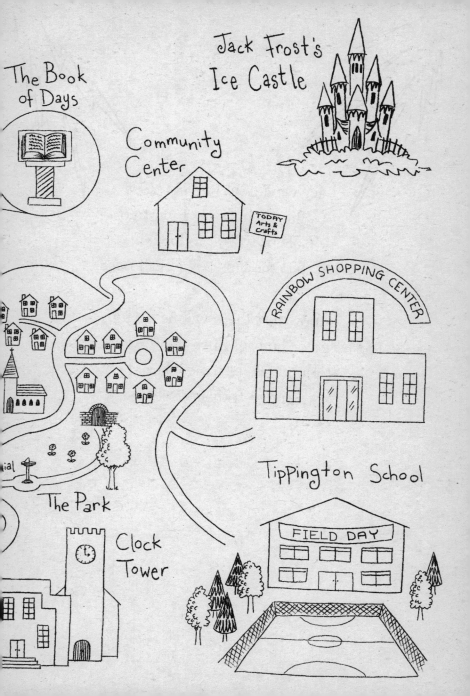

Icy wind now fiercely blow!
To the Time Tower I must go.
Goblins will all follow me
And steal the Fun Day Flags I need.

I know that there will be no fun,
For fairies or humans once the flags are gone.
Storm winds, take me where I say.
My plan for trouble starts today!

Contents

Cooking Up a Storm

"Here's the recipe," Rachel Walker said, showing the cookbook to her best friend, Kirsty Tate. "Don't they look delicious?"

Kirsty looked at the picture and nodded. "I love gingerbread men!" she said.

"Gran always bakes gingerbread cookies for my birthday," Rachel explained. "I thought we could make some for her, since she's coming over today." She laughed as her shaggy dog, Buttons, trotted into the kitchen and looked up at the two girls hopefully. "Buttons likes them, too!"

At that moment, Mrs. Walker, Rachel's mom, followed Buttons into the room.

"Gran will be here soon," she said. "We'd better get started, girls. I'll find the cookie cutter. You two gather all the ingredients."

"OK, Mom," Rachel agreed. "I'll get the eggs. Kirsty, could you get the flour? It's in that cabinet near the sink."

Rachel opened the fridge and Kirsty went to find the flour. Mrs. Walker searched through the drawers for the cookie cutter.

"Mom, we don't have any eggs," Rachel called, her head still inside the fridge.

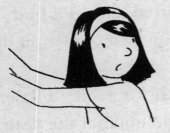

"And there isn't any flour in this cabinet," added Kirsty, scooting jars and boxes aside to check. "That's funny," Mrs. Walker said, shaking her head. "I thought we had plenty of both. And I'm sure I saw the cookie cutter only a few days ago." She frowned. "Maybe it went up to the attic in that box of kitchen equipment we don't use anymore. I'll go and check."

"We're not doing very well, are we?" Rachel sighed as her mom left the room. "This isn't any fun at all."

"You know why, don't you?" Kirsty pointed out. "It's because it's Friday, and

Felicity the Friday Fairy's flag is still missing!"

Rachel and Kirsty shared a special, magical secret. They had become friends with the fairies and were helping their tiny friends find the missing Fun Day Flags! Without the flags, the seven Fun Day Fairies couldn't recharge their wands with the wonderful magic that made every day of the week fun. And without that magic, the human world was blah and boring.

The flags had been stolen from Fairyland by nasty Jack Frost and his mean goblins. But Jack Frost had quickly become annoyed when the flags' magic made the goblins stop working. With the flags around, they only wanted to have fun and play pranks. So Jack Frost cast a powerful spell that sent the flags spinning into the human world.

"You're right, Kirsty,"
Rachel agreed. "Oh, I hope we find Felicity's flag before the goblins do!"

The goblins had missed having fun so much that they had disobeyed Jack Frost. They escaped from Fairyland and followed the flags into the human world! But Rachel and Kirsty had managed to get the better of the goblins so far, and they'd already returned the Monday, Tuesday, Wednesday, and Thursday flags to the fairies.

"We'll do our best," Kirsty replied firmly. "The Fun Day Fairies are counting on us."

Suddenly, the doorbell rang. "That must be Gran!" Rachel exclaimed.

The two girls hurried down the hall, and Rachel opened the front door. As she did, a strong gust of wind pushed the door wide open.

"Hello, girls," Gran said, smiling. "I've had a nice walk over here, but it's rather windy."

"Hi, Gran," Rachel replied, beaming as her grandma gave her a big hug. "Come in."

"Hello," said Kirsty warmly.

"You must be Kirsty!" Gran declared, giving Kirsty a hug, too. "Do call me Gran, dear.

I've heard so much about you, I feel like I know you already!" Kirsty smiled. "OK, Gran!" she agreed.

"It's very odd," Rachel's grandma continued as she stepped into the hall. "While I was walking here, I had the strangest feeling that I was being followed, but when I looked, there was nobody behind me." She laughed and shook her head. "I must be imagining things!"

Rachel closed the door as her grandma
unbuttoned her coat and hung it up in
the closet. As Gran turned back to the
girls, Rachel noticed a beautiful purple
scarf knotted around her neck. The silky
material looked familiar, and Rachel
frowned.

"That's a pretty scarf, Gran," she said.
"Have you worn it before?"

"No, I just bought it yesterday at a secondhand store," Gran explained, untying the scarf. "I love the lilac color and the sun pattern. Look!"

She shook the scarf out and held it up. Rachel and Kirsty glanced at each other in amazement.

It was the missing Fun Day Flag!

A Suspicious Salesman

"It's beautiful," Rachel said to her grandma.

"Yes, it is," Kirsty agreed. She winked at her friend as Gran tied the scarf back around her neck.

Just then, Rachel's mom hurried down the stairs. "Hello, Mom," she said, kissing Gran on the cheek. Then she turned to

Rachel and Kirsty. "Sorry, girls, I couldn't find the cookie cutter in the attic. I'll have to look in the kitchen again."

Rachel was so excited she could hardly wait until her mom and her grandma had walked into the kitchen and out of earshot.

"Kirsty, we've already found the Friday flag!" she whispered, beaming with joy. "I can hardly believe it!"

"You mean the flag found us," Kirsty pointed out. "What should we do now? We can't just take the scarf off your grandma!"

Rachel thought for a moment. "You're right, but the flag's safe for now," she replied. "We'll just have to wait for Felicity to arrive."

"Meanwhile, we can't let the flag out of our sight," Kirsty said anxiously. "There may be goblins around."

Rachel nodded. Quickly, the two girls hurried into the kitchen, where Rachel's grandma was proudly showing the scarf to Mrs. Walker.

"We were going to make gingerbread men for a snack, Gran," Rachel

explained. "But we couldn't find any
flour or eggs."

"Or the cookie cutter," added Kirsty.

"Oh, well. Buttons needs a walk,
anyway," said Mrs. Walker. "I'll take
him out and pick up all the things we

need at the same time."

"OK, Mom," replied
Rachel. "Buttons!"
She took Buttons's
leash off the hook
by the back door,
and Buttons began
jumping around
excitedly, swishing his long furry tail.

"I won't be long," Mrs. Walker said,
picking up her coat. "Maybe you girls
could offer our guest a drink while
I'm out."

"What would you like, Gran?" asked
Rachel, as Mrs. Walker and Buttons left
the house.

"Oh, a glass of juice would be nice,
dear. Thank you,"
Gran replied.

While Gran
went and sat
down in the living
room, Rachel and
Kirsty got the juice
out of the fridge.

"I wonder when
Felicity will get
here," Kirsty said
as they put the juice and three glasses on
a tray.

"I'm sure she'll arrive before Gran goes
home," replied Rachel. "If not, we'll have

to think of a reason to borrow the scarf
and take it back to Fairyland ourselves!"

Rachel carried the tray to the living
room, and Kirsty went ahead to open the
door for her. As Kirsty did, she glanced
over at the window and gasped! A mean,
green face was staring at them through
the glass. It was a goblin!

Rachel had put the tray down and was pouring Gran a glass of juice. She saw Kirsty staring at the window and looked over herself, catching a glimpse of the goblin just before he dodged out of sight. The girls glanced at each other anxiously.

"We're just going to clean up the kitchen, Gran," Rachel said breathlessly. She and Kirsty hurried out into the hall.

"Your grandma said she thought she was being followed — it must have been that goblin!" Kirsty whispered. "He's after the Fun Day Flag!"

"I wish Buttons was here," said Rachel, biting her lip. "The goblins are scared of dogs. He'd have kept them away."

"There could be more than one goblin, too," said Kirsty. "What do we do?"

But before they could decide, the doorbell rang. Kirsty and Rachel jumped.

"Mom can't be back already," Rachel said with a frown. "Anyway, she probably took her key. I wonder who it is?"

The girls went down the hall and opened the front door cautiously. There, on the doorstep, was a very

strange-looking man. He was short, but
was wearing an extremely long coat,
along with sunglasses and a big hat.
He held a bunch of orange marigolds
in his hand.

"I'm selling flowers," the man said in a
rough, gruff voice. "Do you want some?
They're very cheap!"

Rachel and Kirsty stared at the short salesman. Kirsty could see a long green nose poking out from under the hat, and Rachel could see big, green feet sticking out from under the hem of the coat. The girls looked at each other and nodded. The salesman was a goblin!

"Look, beautiful flowers!" the goblin said impatiently, thrusting the flowers under the girls' noses.

Rachel could see that some of the flowers still had roots attached to the stems. She realized that the goblin had just torn them up from the front yard!

"Will you buy them?" the goblin asked, hopping eagerly from one foot to the other. "All I want in return is one lilac scarf! Just one teeny-weeny little scarf, that's all! But it must be lilac. With a sun pattern on it!"

Rachel put her hands on her hips and stared hard at the goblin. "You're not fooling us for one minute, Mr. Goblin!" she said firmly. "And my dad's going to be really annoyed that you've been pulling up his marigolds!"

The goblin scowled, threw the flowers at Kirsty, and ran off down the path as fast as he could, almost tripping over the hem of his coat.

"I managed to catch most of the flowers!" Kirsty said, picking up one that had fallen on the step. "Maybe we can put them in a vase for your mom."

"We're going to have to protect Gran from the goblins!" Rachel said, closing the door.

Kirsty nodded. "I hope Felicity gets here soon," she added.

At that moment, a burst of magical purple sparkles swirled from the bright orange marigolds in Kirsty's hand. Then, a tiny fairy popped her head out from between two of the flowers and waved at the girls.

"It's Felicity the Friday Fairy," cried Rachel. "She's here!"

Goblins After Gran!

Felicity fluttered out from the bunch
of flowers, lilac sparkles and orange
marigold petals drifting around her.
She wore a purple dress with long,
bell-shaped sleeves, a lilac belt with a
heart-shaped buckle, and knee-length
purple boots.

"Hello, girls," Felicity said eagerly.

"Do you know where my flag is? The Book of Days said you would."

The Book of Days was in Fairyland. It was looked after by Francis the frog, the Royal Time Guard. Every morning he checked the book to make sure that he put the correct Fun Day Flag at the top of the flagpole on the Fairyland Time Tower. Ever since the flags had disappeared, poems had been showing up in the Book of Days. Each poem gave clues to where the flags might be.

Felicity flicked back her curly blonde hair and recited:

"The girls will know its hiding place,
The trick will be to keep it safe,
Once the flag is in your care,
Beware the goblins everywhere!"

"Yes, we do know where the flag is, Felicity," Kirsty said quickly.

"Hooray!" Felicity cried, twirling happily in midair. "I can't wait to see my beautiful flag again. Where is it?"

"It's around my grandma's neck," Rachel explained. "She's wearing it as a scarf!"

"But there are goblins here, too," added Kirsty. "We don't know how many."

Felicity looked serious. "Girls, I think there could be lots of goblins! I saw two of them hanging around by the back door."

"Oh no!" Rachel gasped, looking worried. "That's where Buttons's dog door is. The goblins are small enough to get into the house that way!"

Felicity and Kirsty looked concerned.

"Quick, we have to find out if they're in the house!" Felicity said anxiously.

The girls rushed through the house to the back door, with Felicity zooming along behind them. They reached it just in time to see two goblins quietly creeping into the living room.

"Gran's in there alone!" whispered Rachel.

"With the flag," groaned Kirsty. "We have to go after them!"

Kirsty, Rachel, and Felicity dashed through the living room door. Gran was sitting on the sofa, finishing her juice, and the goblins were peeking over the back of the sofa. They were whispering to each other and pointing at Gran's scarf.

Gran put down her empty glass and reached for a magazine from the coffee table. She sat back and began flipping through the pages. Then, before the girls could do anything, one goblin climbed onto the shoulders of the other and slowly reached out to pull the flag from around Gran's neck.

"Oh no, you don't!" Rachel said loudly.

Gran looked startled and dropped the magazine. The goblins both jumped in fright and fell over, the top one tumbling off the shoulders of the other. Glaring at

the girls, both goblins got to their feet
and began dusting themselves off.

Felicity landed on Kirsty's shoulder and
hid behind her hair as the girls hurried
into the room.

Meanwhile, Rachel's grandma was
looking confused. "What's the matter,
dear?" she asked. "Why don't you want
me to read that magazine?"

"Uh . . . um . . ." Rachel stammered, trying to think of something to say.

"Rachel just meant that she wanted to hand the magazine to you," Kirsty said quickly. "She didn't want you to have to get up from the sofa."

Gran smiled. "I'm not so old that I can't get a magazine for myself!" She laughed as Rachel carefully gave the magazine back to her. "But thank you for being thoughtful."

As Gran flipped through the magazine, Rachel glanced over at the goblins. "I think we should get my

grandma out of the house," she
whispered to Kirsty. "We have to keep
her away from the goblins."

Kirsty nodded in agreement.

"Gran, would you like to go out and
see the yard?"
Rachel asked.
"The flowers
are so pretty,
and we
bought a new
birdbath last
week."

"I'd love to,
dear," Gran
replied.

Rachel
opened the
French doors

and they all went outside. It was still very windy, but the patio was sheltered and it was nice and warm in the sun.

"Remember to watch out for goblins everywhere!" Felicity whispered in Kirsty's ear.

Kirsty nodded to let the fairy know that she'd heard her.

"There's the new birdbath," Rachel said, pointing to the middle of the grassy yard.

"It looks lovely," Gran said admiringly. "And aren't these marigolds beautiful?"

she added, stopping as they walked across the patio to admire the bright orange flowers.

All of a sudden, Kirsty caught a flash of movement out of the corner of her eye. She looked around. The Walkers' clothesline stretched behind them and ran the whole length of the yard. A goblin was whizzing along the line, hanging onto it with his big, green hands as he slid along! And he was heading straight toward Rachel's grandma, his knobby, long fingers reaching out to grab the Friday flag!

Disaster Strikes!

Rachel spotted the goblin, too. She glanced at Kirsty, her eyes wide with worry.

Kirsty knew they had to do something — and fast. "Oh, look!" she exclaimed loudly. "Is that a baby robin drinking from the birdbath?"

"Really?" Gran said. She forgot all about the flowers and headed across the yard toward the birdbath, just as the goblin sailed past and reached for the flag. He missed completely! Unable to stop himself, he whizzed to the end of the clothesline and fell headfirst into a thick shrub.

"I can't see the baby robin," Rachel said quickly. She could hear the goblin moaning and muttering behind her, and she didn't want her grandma to notice. "But isn't the birdbath pretty, Gran? Look at this engraved pattern on the side."

"And look at the beautiful dahlias at the other end of the yard," Kirsty added.

Gran looked interested, and the girls quickly led her away from the goblin.

"Good job," Felicity whispered in Kirsty's ear.

"I just wonder how many more goblins are lurking around," Kirsty whispered back.

As they walked along the yard,
away from the sheltered patio,
the wind grew stronger.
The big beech tree was
swaying as they
passed underneath
it, and Rachel
could see a long
green branch
hanging down.

*The wind must
have broken one of
the branches*, she
thought. But then
Rachel realized it
wasn't a branch at
all. It was a goblin
hanging upside-down,
waiting to grab Gran's scarf!

His eyes were shining greedily
as Gran walked closer
and closer.
Rachel desperately
looked over her
shoulder at Kirsty
and Felicity, and
pointed to the
goblin.
Immediately,
Felicity popped
out from behind
Kirsty's hair and
waved her wand.
A few lilac sparkles
whizzed toward
Gran and drifted
around the purse she was
carrying. Suddenly, the

purse fell out of Gran's hand and onto the path.

"Oh my!" Gran exclaimed. "How clumsy of me!" She bent to pick up her bag at the same time that the goblin made a grab for the flag. The goblin missed. He muttered to himself as he swung to and fro. Then, glaring at Felicity and the girls, he pulled himself back up into the tree and out of sight. Felicity smiled and flew over to hide in Rachel's pocket.

"Thank you, Felicity," Rachel said in a low voice while Kirsty pointed out the

bright red dahlias
to Gran.

"The flag isn't
safe while there
are so many
goblins around,"
Felicity said with a frown. "We have to
get it from your grandma so I can take it
safely back to Fairyland!"

Rachel smiled as an idea popped into
her head. "Gran, I really love your new
scarf," she said. "Could I look at it
again, please?"

"Of course," Gran said. She untied the
scarf and held it out to Rachel. But as
she did, a strong gust of wind whipped it
out of her hand. Rachel reached out for
it but missed, and the flag danced away
on the breeze. In another moment, the

wind had carried it around the side of the house.

"Oh no!" Gran exclaimed.

"We'll get it!" Rachel gasped. She and Kirsty ran off as fast as they could, with Felicity still safe in Rachel's pocket. Without looking back, they left Gran to enjoy the flowers.

"I can hear a goblin cackling," Kirsty groaned as they rushed around the side

of the house and paused behind a
large bush.

The girls and
Felicity peeked
around the bush.
A big goblin was
tying Gran's scarf
around his neck.
He laughed as he
admired his reflection
in the glass of the side door.

"We're lucky your grandma can't see
this side of the house from the yard,"
Kirsty whispered.

Rachel nodded. "We have to get the
flag back!" she said softly. "But how?"

Time for a Trick

Felicity and the girls watched the goblin happily tying and untying the scarf in lots of different ways. He wrapped it around his head like a turban. Then he knotted it like a tie, and put it over his shoulders like a shawl, giggling the whole time.

"He's having tons of fun," Kirsty
whispered. Felicity and Rachel nodded.
The flag was magic, and it made
everything fun. Then Kirsty caught her
breath. "Oh!" she gasped. "I've got
an idea!"

"What?" Felicity and Rachel asked.

"If we can fool the goblin into thinking
that the flag isn't fun anymore, he won't
want it!" Kirsty explained.

"That makes sense," Rachel agreed. "But how can we do that?"

Kirsty thought for a moment. "I bet the goblin wouldn't like it if he thought the flag was turning him purple!" she exclaimed, her eyes twinkling.

"You're right. Goblins love to be green," Felicity declared. "And I can change his reflection with my fairy magic." She laughed. "Come and watch the fun!" And, with that, Felicity waved her wand, showering the girls in sparkling lilac fairy dust.

In the blink of an eye, the girls
became fairies with glittering wings on
their backs. They fluttered up into the
air, and Felicity led them toward
the house. She motioned for them to stop
behind the goblin.

He was now tying the scarf around his head so that he looked like a pirate. He chuckled happily. Felicity waved her wand again, and Rachel and Kirsty smiled as the goblin's reflection in the glass door turned exactly the same lilac color as the flag.

"Don't I look handsome?" the goblin said proudly, admiring himself in the glass. Then he looked more closely at his reflection and gave a shriek of horror. "I'm purple!" he yelled. "Help! I've turned the same color as the flag!"

Felicity and the girls hovered behind him, trying not to laugh out loud.

"I don't want to be purple," the goblin groaned. "Goblins are green, not purple."

Felicity tapped the goblin on the  shoulder with her wand. "It's the flag," she said, pointing at his head. "The magic's not working properly." Rachel laughed and pointed at the goblin. "You do look funny," she said. "I've never seen a purple goblin before!"

The goblin looked annoyed.

"Being purple isn't any fun, is it?" said
Kirsty sympathetically.

"No, it isn't!" the goblin muttered, and
he pulled the flag off his head and threw
it on the ground.

Immediately, Felicity and the girls
zoomed down to the flag. With a twirl
of Felicity's wand, the flag became
its tiny, Fairyland size, and Rachel
scooped it up.

But just then, the goblin glanced down at his arms, and his eyes almost popped out of his head. "I'm still green!" he gasped, looking from his arms to the glass door. "It's only my reflection that's

purple!" He began jumping up and down in rage. "You tricked me!"

"We'd better get out of here," Felicity said quickly, as the goblin rushed toward them, grasping for the flag.

Friday Fun!

At that moment, they all heard a
friendly bark.

Woof! Woof!

"That's Buttons!" Rachel cried, as they
also heard the front gate open and close.
"Mom's back!"

The goblin looked terrified. With a
squeal of horror, he dove headfirst into

a nearby lavender bush and disappeared. Kirsty, Rachel, and Felicity couldn't help laughing.

"I think we've probably seen the last of all the goblins, now that Buttons is home," said Kirsty, grinning.

"Thank you so much, girls," Felicity said gratefully as Rachel gave her the Friday flag. "Now I'll be able to take my flag back to Fairyland and recharge my Fun Day magic!"

Rachel and Kirsty nodded happily. They knew that once Francis had raised the Friday flag up the flagpole in the Time Tower, the sun's rays would strike the sparkly material. The rays would then shine directly down into the courtyard to charge Felicity's wand with special magic, so she could make Fridays full of fun!

"Girls!" Rachel's mom called. "Where are you?"

"You'd better go," said Felicity. "But before you do . . ." She twirled her wand, and an exact copy of the Friday flag instantly appeared in Rachel's hand.

"It's for your grandma," Felicity
explained. "It's exactly the same as my
flag, except that it's not magic, of course!
Now good-bye, girls."

Rachel and Kirsty waved as the little
fairy vanished in a swirl of lilac dust.
Then they hurried back to the patio,
where Rachel's mom had joined Gran.
Buttons came running to meet them.

"Oh, you caught my scarf!" Gran declared happily. "Thank you, girls. It's so pretty, I wouldn't want to lose it." Gran tied the scarf firmly around her neck, and they all went inside.

"I bought some jelly beans and chocolate chips to decorate the gingerbread men," said Mrs. Walker as they entered the kitchen. "But I couldn't find a cookie cutter at the general store. We'll just have to make gingerbread cakes, instead."

But Rachel had just noticed a few lilac
sparkles drifting around one of the
kitchen drawers. Her heart pounding
with excitement, she pulled it open.

Four sparkling
silver cookie
cutters lay in the
drawer in front
of her. One was
in the shape of
a fairy, one a
castle, one
a toadstool
house, and the
fourth a
winged horse.

"Look at these!" Rachel said happily,
placing them one by one on the kitchen
counter.

Kirsty's eyes opened wide. "Felicity
must have recharged her Fun Day magic
already!" she
whispered,
picking up the
horse-shaped
cookie cutter.
"Look, Rachel,
this is just like
Pegasus. Do you
remember
meeting him
when we found
Lucy's magic diamond?"

Rachel nodded. "Now we can have
some fun of our own!" she said with a
smile.

Meanwhile, Mrs. Walker looked
bewildered. "I don't remember buying

those," she said. "But aren't they cute? A fairy and a winged horse. How magical."

"I'm looking forward to eating a gingerbread fairy," Gran agreed with a smile. "It'll be a nice change from a boring old gingerbread man!"

Rachel beamed at Kirsty as they began to mix the ingredients together.

"We can almost make a whole gingerbread Fairyland," she whispered, "thanks to Felicity's Fun Day magic!"

"And there are only two more Fun Day Flags to find before I go home on Sunday," said Kirsty. "I really hope we find them before the goblins do!"

RAINBOW magic ™™

THE FUN DAY FAIRIES

Megan, Tara, Willow, Thea, and
Felicity all have their flags back. Now
Rachel and Kirsty need to help

Sienna
the Saturday
Fairy!

Fantastic Fashion

"You look beautiful," Rachel Walker said, looking at her friend Kirsty Tate.

"So do you," Kirsty replied. The two girls grinned at each other. Kirsty was staying with Rachel during their school vacation, and they'd been doing all sorts of fun things together. But today, Saturday, was going to be especially exciting. Rachel's cousin, Caroline, was opening a new clothing store in the Rainbow Shopping Center. Caroline had planned a fashion show featuring some of the store's cutest clothes. Even better, she had asked Rachel and Kirsty to be two of her models.

Kirsty and Rachel followed Caroline, both feeling tingly with excitement. The fashion show was going to take place in the lobby of the mall. There was a backstage area with large screens and partitions that made different rooms, and it seemed like a maze. "First, I'll show you the stage," Caroline said. The stage was long and narrow, with lots of bright spotlights — just like a real catwalk!

There were two hidden entrances. As the girls peeked out from behind the curtain backstage, they saw a cameraman setting up his equipment.

Kirsty and Rachel could see that some people were already sitting in the rows of seats on either side of the catwalk. Unfortunately, none of them looked excited to be there. In fact, most of them seemed a little bored!

Rachel shot Kirsty a look. Both girls knew exactly why the audience looked so down — it was because the Saturday Fun Flag was missing!

Come flutter by Butterfly Meadow!

Butterfly Meadow #1: Dazzle's First Day
Dazzle is a new butterfly, fresh out of her cocoon. She doesn't know how to fly, and she's all alone! But Butterfly Meadow could be just what Dazzle is looking for.

Butterfly Meadow #2: Twinkle Dives In
Twinkle is feisty, fun, and always up for an adventure. But the nearby pond holds much more excitement than she expected!

www.scholastic.com